Bedrock Press™
ATLANTA

Published by Bedrock Press
An imprint of Turner Publishing, Inc.
A Subsidiary of Turner Broadcasting System, Inc.
1050 Techwood Drive, N. W.
Atlanta, Georgia 30318

Printed in the U. S. A.
First Edition 10 9 8 7 6 5 4 3 2 1
ISBN 1-878685-67-8
Library of Congress Catalog
Card Number 93-61334

Distributed by Andrews and McMeel
A Universal Press Syndicate Company
4900 Main Street, Kansas City,
Missouri 64112

DK DIRECT LIMITED
Managing Art Editor Eljay Crompton
Senior Editor Rosemary Mc Cormick
Consultant Dr. Michael Benton
Writer Rachel Wright
Illustrators Hanna-Barbera, Inc.,
Jim Robins, Elsa Godfrey
Designers Diane Klein, Marianne Markham

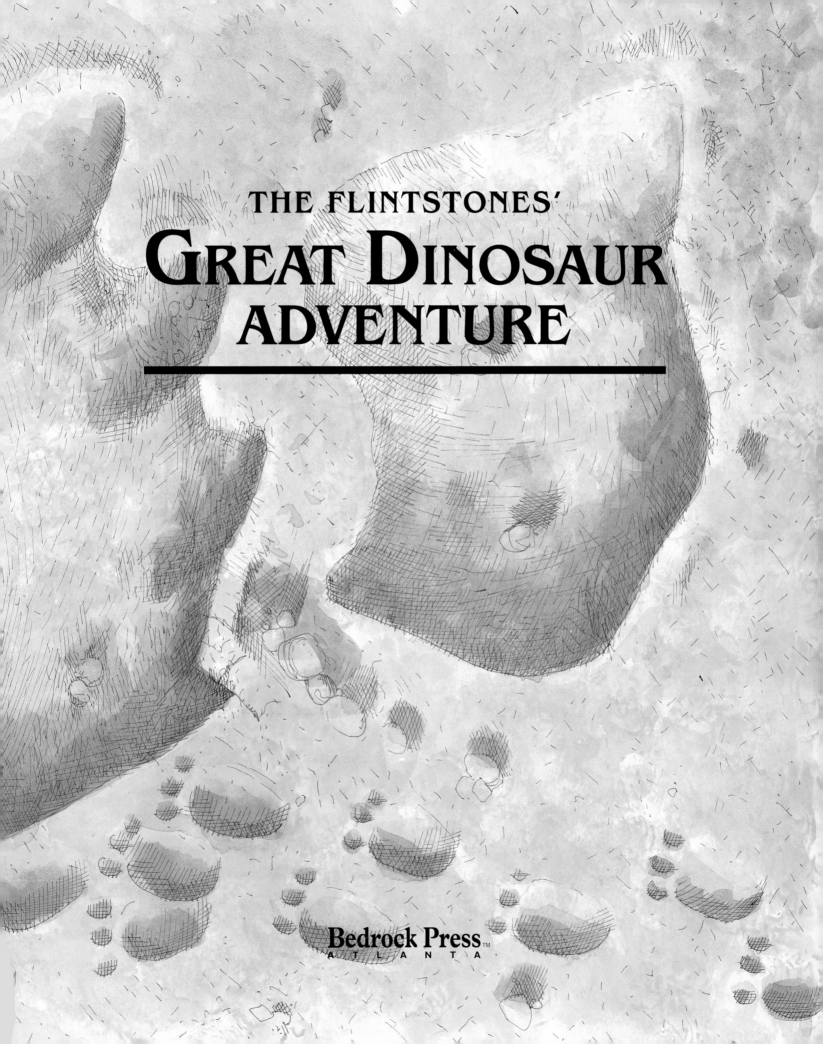

THE FLINTSTONES'
GREAT DINOSAUR
ADVENTURE

Bedrock Press™
ATLANTA

"DEAR READER"

This book has been created especially
for you. It's guaranteed to provide fun,
adventure, and fabulous nuggets of
information. And the fascinating
facts – just like dinosaurs – come in
all different shapes and sizes. On
this time-travel tour back to the Land of
the Dinosaurs, the Flintstones will be
your trusty guides. We hope you enjoy
this exciting adventure, and we look
forward to having you join us on
another Fantastic Discovery.

CONTENTS

Are you ready to go time-traveling? If so, step into your time machine and set the dial to 230 million years ago – to the days when dinosaurs first appeared. And while we are there, we can visit our friends the Flintstones. Back then, the land was joined together into one mass called Pangaea. Early dinosaurs were able to migrate to continents now separated by water.

Land of the Dinos
In early dinosaur times, much of the Earth was covered in desert, but there were swampy areas.

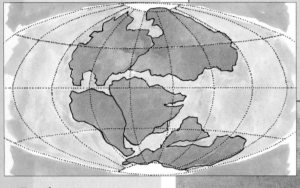

By the time dinosaurs died out, Pangaea, or the Super Continent, had split up. The pieces of land we call continents were beginning to move toward their present positions.

CHARACTERISTICS: Special qualities or features that distinguish one thing from another.

CONTINENT: One of Earth's seven main landmasses.

MIGRATE: To move from one country, region, or place, to another.

Mammal History
Today's mammals are hairy animals that give birth to live babies and feed them with their own milk. They are descended from mammal-like reptiles like these TRAVERSODON. Big mammals didn't develop until after the dinosaurs had become extinct.

Dinosaur Weather

Millions of years ago, the weather was hot and dry everywhere. Over time the climate began to change, and by the end of the dinosaurs' reign, some parts of the world had cooled down.

Ancient Insects

Even in dinosaur times there were creepy-crawly insects and spiders. There were scorpions and some very large dragonflies, too.

Different kinds of creatures, including dinosaurs, have lived at different times in Earth's history. One reason for this is that as the landscape and climate changes, so does life on Earth. This diagram shows the three main dinosaur periods – 1. Triassic; 2. Jurassic; 3. Cretaceous – as well as life before and after the dinosaurs.

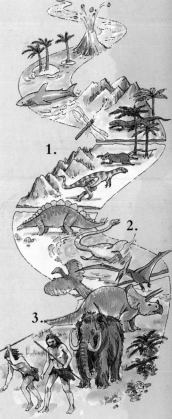

1.

2.

3.

The Dinosaur Family

Dinosaurs were basically reptiles. That's why they had many reptile-like features and characteristics. Dinosaurs laid eggs, as do most reptiles, and they had scaly skin. But many reptiles, such as this DIMETRODON, appeared on Earth millions of years before dinosaurs.

The first dinosaurs evolved about 230 million years ago, in the Triassic Period. Some sped along on their back legs, while others plodded about on all fours. The second era – beginning 205 million years ago and called the Jurassic Period – saw the arrival of dinosaurs with very long necks. But perhaps the strangest-looking dinosaurs, such as PARASAUROLOPHUS, appeared in the third or Cretaceous Period 150 million years ago.

In 1972, in Colorado, the bones of a huge SAUROPOD were discovered. Its shoulder blade is longer than a person. When it was first discovered it was given the name Supersaurus!

This is one of the tiniest dinosaur discoveries of all. This baby dinosaur skeleton measures about four inches across.

ERA: The period of time during which something or someone exists.

EVOLVE: To unfold, or develop gradually.

HOLLOW: Having nothing, or only air, inside.

PROTECT: To shelter or shield from danger; to defend.

Saying Hello
PARASAUROLOPHUS had a long, hollow horn on the top of its head. It probably used this horn to make honking noises, to let others know where it was.

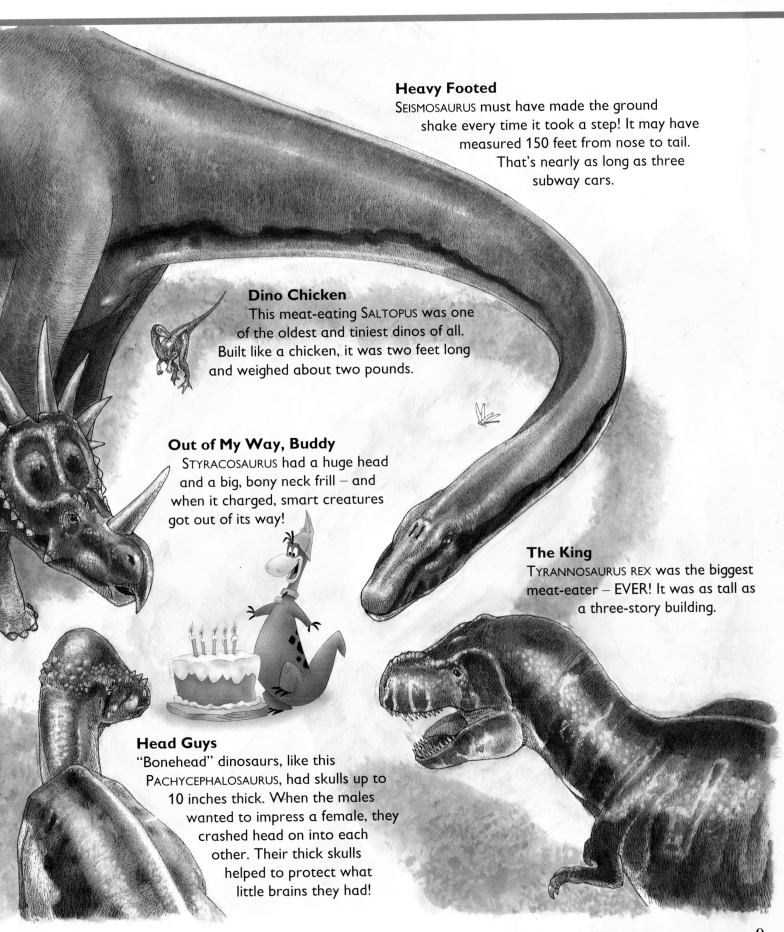

Heavy Footed
SEISMOSAURUS must have made the ground shake every time it took a step! It may have measured 150 feet from nose to tail. That's nearly as long as three subway cars.

Dino Chicken
This meat-eating SALTOPUS was one of the oldest and tiniest dinos of all. Built like a chicken, it was two feet long and weighed about two pounds.

Out of My Way, Buddy
STYRACOSAURUS had a huge head and a big, bony neck frill – and when it charged, smart creatures got out of its way!

The King
TYRANNOSAURUS REX was the biggest meat-eater – EVER! It was as tall as a three-story building.

Head Guys
"Bonehead" dinosaurs, like this PACHYCEPHALOSAURUS, had skulls up to 10 inches thick. When the males wanted to impress a female, they crashed head on into each other. Their thick skulls helped to protect what little brains they had!

DINOSAUR DIET

All creatures' teeth are designed to help them chew the foods they like to eat. Meat-eating dinos had sharp teeth for tearing. Many plant-eaters had special teeth for grinding.

Human molar

Lion's slicing tooth

TROODON tooth

MEGALOSAURUS tooth

Not all dinosaurs were meat-eaters. Some were plant-eaters that preferred a leafy lunch to a STEGOSAURUS steak – unlike Barney, who would never turn his nose up at a steak! All dinosaurs had teeth or jaws to suit the kinds of food they ate. Those that chewed tough plants had strong teeth and jaws. Those that ate soft shoots had smaller, weaker teeth. Most meat-eating dinosaurs had fangs with jagged edges. And a few had no teeth at all!

One Big Bite
Like other large meat-eaters, this ALLOSAURUS had a huge head, strong legs, and short arms for grasping prey. Its jaws could open wide enough to swallow lumps of meat almost as big as its head!

Pack Hunters
Some hungry meat-eaters hunted in packs. CERATOSAURUS was only about 15 feet long, but a pack of them could bring down much bigger dinosaurs.

Head to Toe
BAROSAURS were long-necked, long-tailed, giant plant-eaters.

Running Scared
Some plant-eaters, such as this group of DRYOSAURS, had long, agile legs to help them race away from meat-eaters. They didn't have front teeth, so they nipped vegetation off the ground with their "beaks."

Bird Lovers
Many lightly built meat-eaters, such as ORNITHOLESTES, chased and killed small lizards and birds. ORNITHOLESTES means "bird robber."

Plant-eaters ate ferns and conifers — such as the spiky monkey puzzle plant on the right.

Some plant-eating dinosaurs swallowed stones to help grind up the tough plants they had eaten, and which lay, undigested, in their stomachs.

AGILE: Able to move quickly and easily.

PACK: A number of animals of the same kind gathered together — especially animals that hunt.

ON THE ATTACK

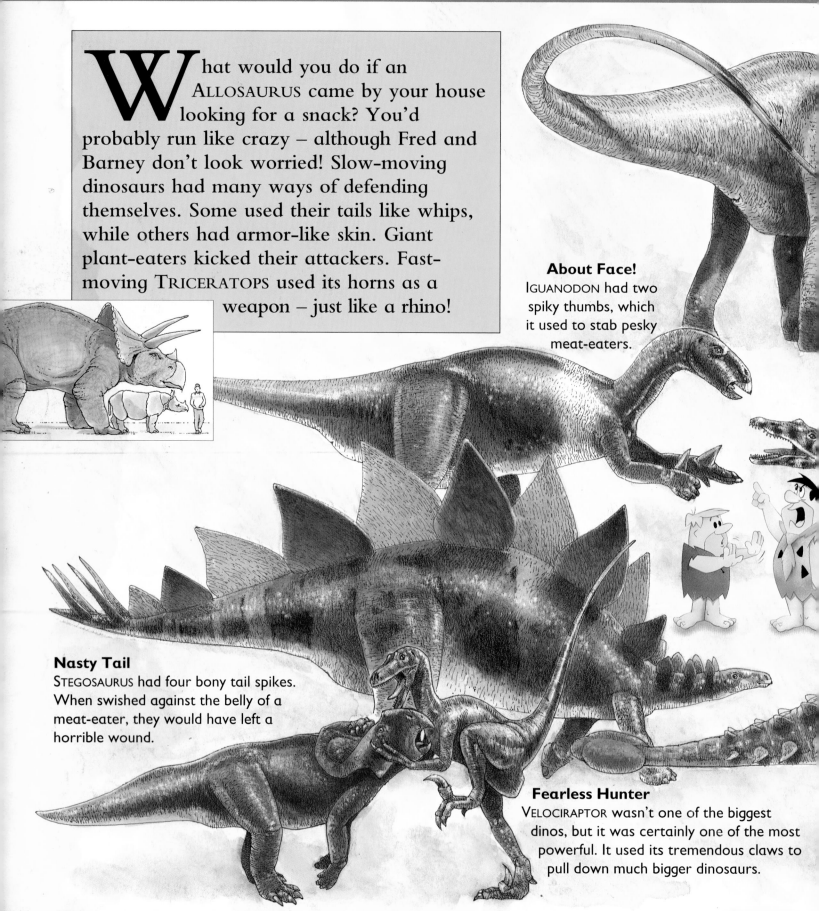

What would you do if an ALLOSAURUS came by your house looking for a snack? You'd probably run like crazy – although Fred and Barney don't look worried! Slow-moving dinosaurs had many ways of defending themselves. Some used their tails like whips, while others had armor-like skin. Giant plant-eaters kicked their attackers. Fast-moving TRICERATOPS used its horns as a weapon – just like a rhino!

About Face!
IGUANODON had two spiky thumbs, which it used to stab pesky meat-eaters.

Nasty Tail
STEGOSAURUS had four bony tail spikes. When swished against the belly of a meat-eater, they would have left a horrible wound.

Fearless Hunter
VELOCIRAPTOR wasn't one of the biggest dinos, but it was certainly one of the most powerful. It used its tremendous claws to pull down much bigger dinosaurs.

Tail Attack

With one lash of its whip-like tail, DIPLODOCUS could have knocked an enemy off its feet. Such a crafty move would have given this dino a chance to escape.

Clever Claws

BARYONYX had great curved claws that were about 12 inches long.

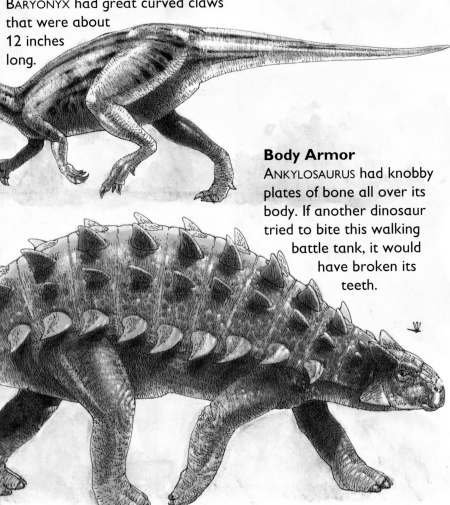

Body Armor

ANKYLOSAURUS had knobby plates of bone all over its body. If another dinosaur tried to bite this walking battle tank, it would have broken its teeth.

The word STEGOSAURUS *means "roof lizard." It got its name because it was once thought that its plates lay flat on its back like tiles on a roof.*

TYRANNOSAURUS REX *is thought to have attacked its prey by running at it with its jaws wide open — ready to take a big bite!*

Like many plant-eating dinosaurs, DIPLODOCUS *stayed together in herds to defend themselves from attack. The young, protected from harm, marched in the middle of the group.*

ARMOR: A covering which protects the body.

KNOBBY: To be covered with rounded lumps.

SMALL-BRAINED BUT SMART

Scientists can tell a dino's brain size by measuring the hole in the skull where the brain would have been.

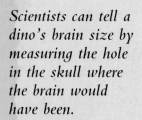

People often think that dinosaurs were dumb because they had tiny brains compared to the size of their bodies. Yet dinosaurs' brains were obviously big enough for their needs because they managed to live on Earth for about 165 million years! What's more, they even found clever ways of heating up and cooling down. Looks like Fred and Barney have found a cool way of dealing with those warm rays!

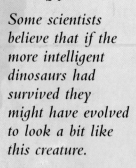

Some scientists believe that if the more intelligent dinosaurs had survived they might have evolved to look a bit like this creature.

MAMMAL: A warm-blooded animal that feeds its young with milk, has a backbone, and usually grows hair or fur.

Turn to the Sun
OURANOSAURUS had a "sail" of skin and spines along its back. When it was cold, it may have stood sideways to the sun, to warm up the blood inside the "sail."

Baby Care
If caring for baby dinos is a sign of intelligence, then HYPSILOPHODONTIDS were pretty smart. They watched over their eggs and carefully arranged them within the nest.

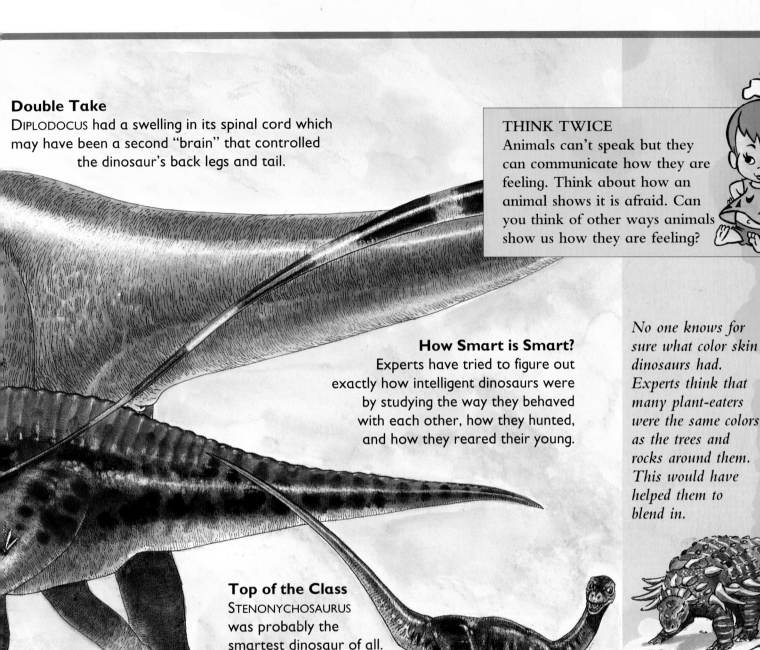

Double Take
DIPLODOCUS had a swelling in its spinal cord which may have been a second "brain" that controlled the dinosaur's back legs and tail.

THINK TWICE
Animals can't speak but they can communicate how they are feeling. Think about how an animal shows it is afraid. Can you think of other ways animals show us how they are feeling?

How Smart is Smart?
Experts have tried to figure out exactly how intelligent dinosaurs were by studying the way they behaved with each other, how they hunted, and how they reared their young.

No one knows for sure what color skin dinosaurs had. Experts think that many plant-eaters were the same colors as the trees and rocks around them. This would have helped them to blend in.

Top of the Class
STENONYCHOSAURUS was probably the smartest dinosaur of all. It was six feet six inches long, and it had a big brain in relation to its body size.

Flying Dinosaurs
Since a fossil of this feathered creature was found, experts think that some dinos had feathers. The feathers must have kept dinos warm, but did they also help them fly?

BEHAVIOR: A way of acting or behaving; actions.

BLEND: To be mixed together so well that things cannot be distinguished.

Dinosaur footprints reveal whether dinosaurs hunted in packs, pairs, or alone.

These footprints were originally thought to be the footprints of giant, prehistoric birds.

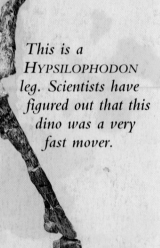

This is a HYPSILOPHODON leg. Scientists have figured out that this dino was a very fast mover.

Have you ever watched a crocodile waddle or a lizard wiggle? Unlike these reptiles, whose legs stick out sideways, dinosaurs had legs that were held under their bodies. This made it easier for them to walk, either on two legs or on four. Most meat-eaters walked on their back legs. Giant plant-eaters moved on all fours so all their limbs supported their great weight. Let's hope BRACHIOSAURUS doesn't squash our friends!

Look Out!
Not all big four-footed dinosaurs were slow plodders. TRICERATOPS could charge along at about 20 mph.

Take a Left
Fast-footed dinos, like HYPSILOPHODON, ran with their tails out-stretched. This helped them to balance — especially when going around corners.

Plodding Along
Like other giant dinos, BRACHIOSAURUS would have broken its legs if it had tried to gallop. With its huge body and narrow feet, it was better suited to walking slowly!

Catching Lunch
Some of the tiniest dinosaurs were very nimble. COMPSOGNATHUS was about the size of a crow. It could scoot along fast enough to catch lizards and insects.

Most reptiles are known as "sprawlers" because their legs stick out at an angle. But dinosaurs, like birds and mammals, had legs tucked beneath their bodies. This helped them support their huge weight.

Some scientists think that dinosaurs may have migrated, seeking warmer temperatures and better food supplies.

Super Speedy
"Ostrich" dinosaurs were the fastest dinosaurs of all. This one, called GALLIMIMUS, may have reached speeds of up to 30 mph. That's about as fast as a horse can gallop.

GALLOP: The fastest gait form of movement in four-footed animals.

REPTILE: One of a group of cold-blooded animals that have backbones and are usually covered with scales.

EGGS, NESTS, AND BABY DINOSAURS

This picture shows how a baby dinosaur would have grown inside its egg.

B aby dinosaurs hatched from eggs. Dinosaur eggs were very small. Even those laid by very big dinosaurs were no more than 12 inches long. This is because the larger an egg grows, the thicker its shell is. If dinosaur eggs had been huge, their shells would not have let enough air through to reach the baby inside. Also, no baby dino would have been strong enough to break out of a big, thick shell.

Human babies are quite small when they are born and grow slowly over about 18 years to their full height and weight.

Watch Out!
TROODONS are thought to have been egg stealers. They had grasping hands that they may have used to steal tasty eggs.

Baby dinos started out really tiny but grew quickly. Some dinosaurs grew to be ten thousand times their original birth size.

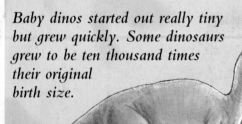

Giving Birth
Some experts think that a few of the larger dinosaurs may have given birth to live babies – but no one knows for sure.

PARENTING:
The methods and techniques used to rear babies.

Caring Mothers
After laying their eggs, some dinosaurs probably left their young to look after themselves. Others, like MAIASAURA, waited for their babies to grow older.

Nesting Time
Every year, MAIASAURA mothers returned to the same nesting places. Their nests held about 25 eggs and were the size of a large paddling pool.

Growing Up
A baby dinosaur grew up fast. By the time it was five or six years old, a MAIASAURA was probably fully grown and ready for its own family.

THINK TWICE
Most reptiles leave their eggs after laying them. When the eggs hatch they are tiny yet exact copies of their parents. Can you guess why mammals stay with their young for so long?

Dinosaurs couldn't fly, but their reptile cousins, the PTEROSAURS, could! While dinosaurs ruled the land, the PTEROSAURS ruled the sky, and groups of marine reptiles, such as PLESIOSAURS, ruled the sea. PTEROSAURS flew on wings of skin. Their bones were full of holes to make them light. The sea reptiles were some of the fiercest water creatures ever – so a fishing trip could have been a little scary!

Little and Large
Some PTEROSAURS were only the size of a sparrow. Others were HUGE. From wingtip to wingtip, this PTERANODON was about the size of a two-seater airplane.

Balancing Act

Many PTEROSAURS had a bony head crest, which may have helped them balance in the air. Others had a long tail with a kite-shaped end that helped them to steer.

LONGISQUAMA was a small reptile that used the long, stiff scales on its back to glide through the air.

Catching Fish

ELASMOSAURUS had four turtle-like flippers and a long bendy neck.

Time to Eat!

TYLOSAURUS was like a giant crocodile with flippers. It pushed itself through the water with its tail. It captured prey by pursuing them and then used its strong teeth for the kill!

QUETZALCOATLUS was the biggest flying animal that ever lived. With its wings outstretched, it measured about 45 feet across.

CONTROL: To have power or authority over; direct.

GLIDE: To move in the air smoothly and easily.

MARINE: Of the sea; found in the sea.

STEER: To direct one's way or course; to guide.

21

FOSSIL FINDS

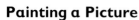

Dragonfly fossil

For a skeleton, or other body part, to survive and become a fossil, it must be covered by layers of sand or mud.

Over time, the layers of sand and mud turn to rock. Parts of the animal decay and are replaced by minerals.

Movements deep beneath the ground cause the skeleton to break up and then to move upward.

Wind and rain wear away the rock and the fossils eventually break through to the surface.

DECAY: To decompose or rot.

REMAINS: Whatever is left over or behind; a dead body.

MINERAL: A natural substance obtained from the ground.

REPLACE: To put something new in the place of.

Painting a Picture

When experts have decided how the bones were once joined together they make a life-size copy of the dinosaur's skeleton. By looking at the model skeleton they can guess where the muscles and other parts of the dinosaur's body went as well.

Nice Try

When dinosaur bones were first discovered, scientists weren't sure how to piece the bones together – so they often got it wrong. This nineteenth century model of an IGUANODON turned out to be quite wrong!

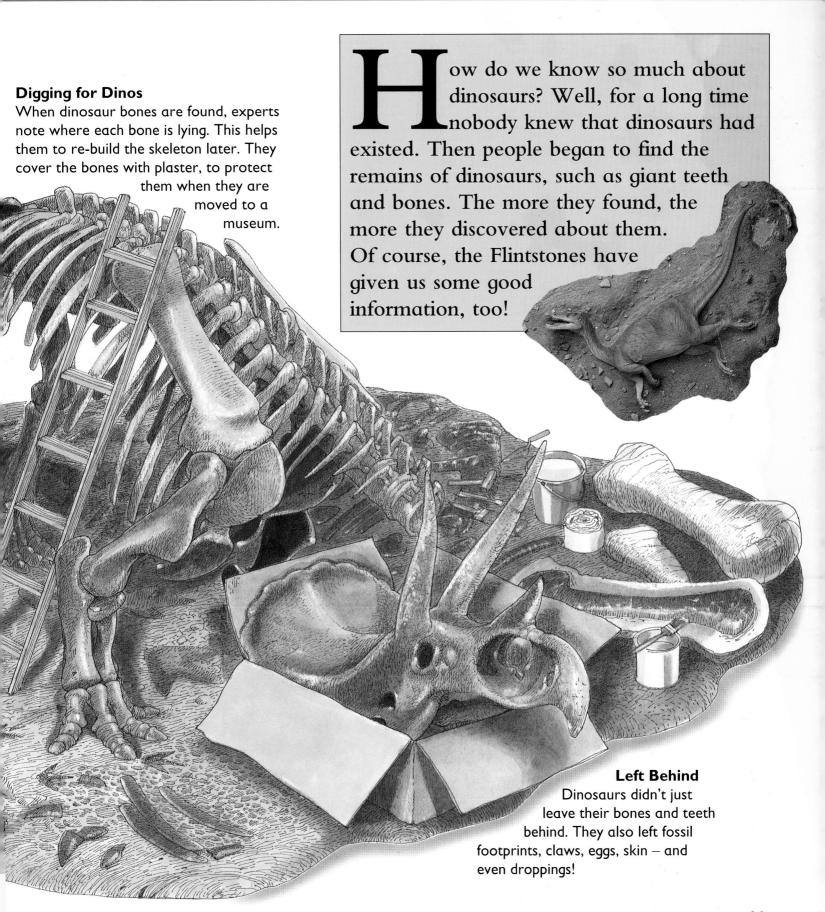

Digging for Dinos
When dinosaur bones are found, experts note where each bone is lying. This helps them to re-build the skeleton later. They cover the bones with plaster, to protect them when they are moved to a museum.

How do we know so much about dinosaurs? Well, for a long time nobody knew that dinosaurs had existed. Then people began to find the remains of dinosaurs, such as giant teeth and bones. The more they found, the more they discovered about them. Of course, the Flintstones have given us some good information, too!

Left Behind
Dinosaurs didn't just leave their bones and teeth behind. They also left fossil footprints, claws, eggs, skin – and even droppings!

THE GREAT DINOSAUR MYSTERY

Some scientists think that caterpillars may have chomped their way through tons of vegetation, leaving less for plant-eaters.

So what happened to the Dinosaurs? The answer is – nobody knows – not even Fred or Barney! Perhaps asteroids from space crashed into the Earth and created a great sooty cloud that blocked out the sun. Without sunlight the plants, and the animals that ate them, died. Or, maybe as Pangaea broke up and the world's weather changed, the climate just got a bit too cold for them.

Some think that dinosaurs were poisoned by new flowering plants.

Takeover Time
With the dinosaurs gone, mammals took over the world. Early mammals ate insects that fed on dead plants, and so an absence of sunlight would not have mattered to them.

ASTEROID: One of thousands of small planetoids that move in orbits mostly between those of Mars and Jupiter.

Staying Power
Whatever happened to the dinosaurs didn't affect mammals, birds, frogs, crocodiles, lizards, and turtles. They are still very much a part of our world today.

Fossil Facts
We know that dinosaurs died out about 65 million years ago because there are no dinosaur fossils in rocks under 65 million years old.

Dusty Death
Scientists think that the asteroid's impact on the Earth sent up a dust-cloud that blocked the sun for many years. Plants died, and then the dinosaurs that fed on them.

The most popular theory is that an asteroid crashed into the Earth at the end of the Cretaceous period. It's impact would have been like 300 million hydrogen bombs exploding!

But dinosaurs may not have left us overnight. As the world's climate cooled, dinosaurs may have slowly disappeared.

THINK TWICE
If you could travel back in time, and meet just one dinosaur, which one would you choose?

BRAINSTORM

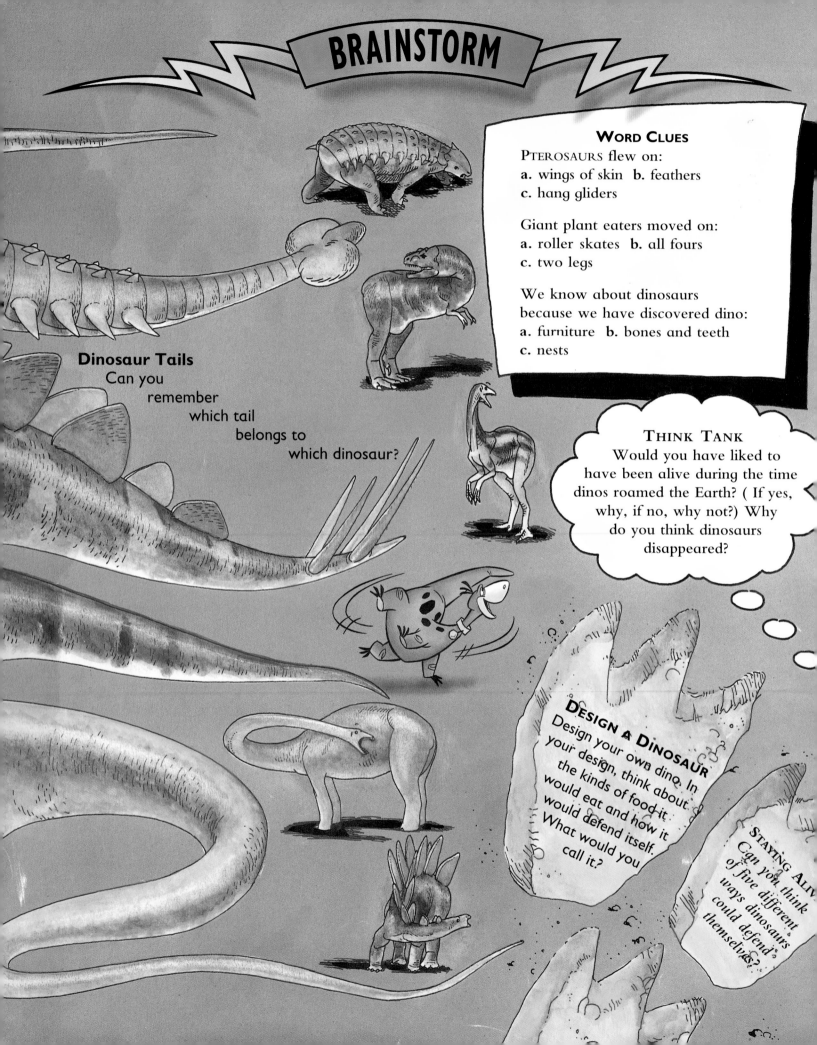

Dinosaur Tails
Can you remember which tail belongs to which dinosaur?

THINK TANK
Would you have liked to have been alive during the time dinos roamed the Earth? (If yes, why, if no, why not?) Why do you think dinosaurs disappeared?

DESIGN A DINOSAUR
Design your own dino. In your design, think about the kinds of food it would eat and how it would defend itself. What would you call it?

STAYING ALIVE
Can you think of five different ways dinosaurs could defend themselves?

QUESTION TIME

When were dinosaurs first thought to have appeared on Earth? When did they disappear?

Why did plant-eaters need to swallow stones?

How was this mean and mighty dinosaur thought to have attacked its prey?

What was the name of the Super Continent of long ago?

If dinosaurs came back to Earth, which ones would be small enough to fit in your closet?

Which dinosaurs were thought to have been egg-stealers?

Name the largest flying reptile that ever lived.

How do we know dinosaurs once lived on Earth?